ERNIE G'S DREAM

THE HIDDEN TRUTH OF WALL STREET

Ernest E Goethe

The characters and events portrayed in this book are fictitious. Any similarity to real persons, living or dead, is coincidental and not intended by the author.

ISBN:9798862310573

Cover design by: Ernest Goethe

CONTENTS

Title Page
Copyright
Introduction
PART 1 1
Chapter 1 2
Chapter 2 6
Chapter 3 10
Chapter 4 12
Chapter 5 16
Chapter 6 20
Chapter 7 23
Chapter 8 27
Chapter 9 31
Chapter 10 35
Chapter 11 38
Chapter 12 41
PART 2 45
Chapter 13 46
Chapter 14 50
Chapter 15 54
Chapter 16 58

Chapter 17 62
Chapter 18 66
Chapter 19 69
Part 3 71
Chapter 20 72
Chapter 21 76
Chapter 22 80
Chapter 23 84
Chapter 24 88
Chapter 25 92
Conclusion 95
About The Author 97

INTRODUCTION

Ever wondered what goes on behind the scenes of Wall Street, that iconic place where dreams of wealth and success are born? Well, so did I. That's why I decided to dive deep into the world of finance and uncover the hidden truths that often stay out of the limelight.

Welcome to "Ernie G's Dream: The Hidden Truth of Wall Street." Now, I'm no financial guru or Wall Street insider; I'm just a regular guy who got curious about what really happens on that bustling street in the heart of New York City. And let me tell you, what I found is nothing short of fascinating. You see, Wall Street is known for its glitz and glamour, the stock market highs and lows that dominate headlines. But there's more to this place than meets the eye. It's a world of high-stakes gambles, incredible success stories, and devastating crashes. It's a place where fortunes are made and lost in the blink of an eye.

In this book, we're going to take a journey together. We'll meet Ernie G, a man who's been through it all. He didn't start out as a Wall Street hotshot. In fact, Ernie had his share of trouble as a young man. But then, something changed. He joined the Navy, served with honor, and emerged with an honorable discharge. With a newfound sense of purpose, Ernie set out to pursue his dreams, only to be met with disappointment and bad news. But here's where the story takes a turn. Ernie discovered that the secret to wealth wasn't in a fancy license or Wall Street's grandeur. The real secret lay in the principles a person lived by.

Once Ernie learned these crucial lessons, he didn't just stop at becoming successful; he became a CEO, a devoted husband, and a community leader. He went from knowing very little about finance to becoming the greatest financier his community had ever produced. The leaders who had led revolutions before him would undoubtedly be proud, and I'm certain they're all cheering with joy from above. So, forget about the fancy suits and the stock tickers for a moment. Join me as we uncover the real story behind Wall Street's façade and the incredible journey of Ernie G. "Ernie G's Dream" isn't about selling you a dream of wealth; it's about revealing the unvarnished truth that lies beneath the financial dreams many of us harbor.

PART 1

RISING DREAMS

CHAPTER 1

CHILDHOOD SHADOWS

The scent of nostalgia hung heavy in the air as I strolled down the streets of Newark, New Jersey. Born and raised in this rebellious city, my roots ran deep in the soil of 570 South 12th Street, right in the heart of the west side. They called it the "numbered blocks," a place where dreams were born, battles were fought, and stories were etched into the very bricks of the neighborhood. Newark had a reputation, not all of it savory; it was known as the car theft capital of the country, but there was more to this city than met the eye.

The numbered blocks had a rich history, like the bloodlines of the families that had lived here for generations. In the shadows of its tenement buildings, Newark had witnessed the rise of rebellion and the fall of giants. It was a place where icons like Malcolm X and Amiri Baraka had left their mark, where jazz notes floated through smoky bars, and where the echoes of protests reverberated through the streets.

As I walked past the corner where a century-old jazz club once stood, I couldn't help but feel the weight of history on my shoulders. Newark had seen it all, and it wasn't just a city; it was a living, breathing entity with a spirit of its own. A place that demanded respect, challenged the status quo, and bred fearless individuals.

Growing up here was like an initiation into a secret society of street smarts and survival skills. The numbered blocks had a way of shaping you, making you tough and resourceful. It wasn't always an easy place to call home, but it was home nonetheless.

In the midst of all this, I, Ernie, stood as a product of my environment. My parents' unhappy marriage had cast a perpetual gloom over our household, but it also fueled my determination to escape this cycle of discontent. My mother, with her unrelenting ambition, had instilled in me the importance of dreaming big, while my father's fearless demeanor had shown me that there was no challenge too great to conquer.

As I continued my journey through the city's history-laden streets, I couldn't help but wonder what the future held for a young man like me, born and bred in the rebellious heart of Newark.

My early years in the numbered blocks were anything but ordinary. The neighborhood had its own rhythm, its own heartbeat, and its own set of rules. It was a place where concrete jungles stretched for miles, alleyways whispered secrets, and fire hydrants provided a reprieve from the sweltering summers.

In those streets, I learned to navigate a world that was equal parts unpredictable and exciting. The numbered blocks were more than just a location; they were a character in the story of my life. Each building, each corner store, and each face told a tale of struggle and survival.

But even in the midst of adversity, there was a vibrant energy that flowed through the neighborhood. It was a place where people looked out for each other, where your neighbor's business was your business, and where the bonds of community ran deep.

However, the backdrop of this tumultuous world was the constant discord within my own home. My parents' unhappy marriage cast a long shadow over my childhood. Their never-ending battles reverberated through the walls, painting our home with a somber hue.

As a child, I yearned for the laughter and harmony that seemed to exist in the lives of my friends, but all I knew were the harsh words and bitter exchanges that left scars on my young heart. My parents, once deeply in love, had become strangers trapped in a cycle of resentment and regret.

My old man, who was not a perfect role model, had one thing going for him that left an indelible mark on my impressionable mind—fearlessness. My father had a swagger, an air of confidence

that seemed to make even the most daunting challenges bow down in surrender. His fearless demeanor was like armor, and I, his wide-eyed apprentice, soaked up his lessons like a sponge.
In a neighborhood where danger often lurked in the shadows, my father's courage was legendary.

He didn't flinch when confronted by adversity, and his boldness was both his greatest strength and his greatest flaw. I admired him for it, even as a child, and it was from him that I inherited my relentless desire to be fearless, no matter the odds. But for all his courage outside the home, my father's fearlessness could do little to mend the toxic atmosphere that had enveloped our family. The relentless battles between my parents created a suffocating cloud of tension that clung to our household. The home that should have been a sanctuary had become a battlefield, and I was caught in the crossfire of their discontent.

Their arguments were like a never-ending storm, raging through the night and into the early hours of morning. The echoes of their bitter exchanges haunted my dreams, and the lines on their faces deepened with each passing day. While my parents' love for me was undeniable, it was their inability to find common ground that became the defining backdrop of my childhood.

My parents' love for me, though often buried beneath layers of resentment and frustration, was undeniable. Despite the tempestuous climate of our household, their affection and concern for their son remained unwavering. They were, in their own way, trying to do right by me, even if it meant navigating the treacherous waters of their failing marriage.

CHAPTER 2

DIVORCE

The story of my parents' divorce is like a dark cloud that hung over my childhood, casting a shadow I couldn't escape. It was a bitterness that seeped into every corner of our lives, turning our home into a battlefield.

It all started with their marriage, a union that seemed doomed from the beginning. My father, a fearless man who was never afraid to take risks, and my mother, a woman with boundless ambition, clashed like oil and water. They were both strong-willed, determined individuals, but their dreams pulled them in different directions.

The bitterness between them grew like a malignant tumor. Every argument, every harsh word, seemed to push them further apart. I watched it unfold, a young boy caught in the crossfire of their anger and resentment. There were no winners in their battles, only casualties, and I felt like the biggest loser of them all. As a child, I couldn't fully comprehend the complexities of their relationship, but I could feel the tension in the air. It was as if the walls of our home absorbed their anger, and I absorbed it too. Their constant bickering became the soundtrack of my childhood, a never-ending loop of hostility.

I was the unwilling witness to their marital breakdown, a spectator to their emotional warfare. I longed for peace, for a home where I didn't have to tiptoe around their explosive arguments. But that dream seemed increasingly elusive with each passing day. Their battles took a toll on my young heart. I carried the weight of their unhappiness on my shoulders, a burden I was ill-equipped to bear. I became a quiet and introspective child, seeking solace in books and daydreams. Fearlessness seemed like a distant concept in a world consumed by fear and anger.
The final blow came when my mother decided to move to Baltimore, a city that might as well have been on the other side of the world. She claimed it was for the sake of her career, but it felt like a deliberate act of separation. My parents' geographical

distance mirrored the emotional chasm that had grown between them.

My mother's departure marked the beginning of an era of loneliness and confusion. I was left in the custody of my father, a man who had always been my hero. But even he couldn't shield me from the pain of losing my mother. The empty spaces in our home echoed with her absence.
My mother's remarriage was the final blow. She introduced me to her new husband, a great man and I learned to love him dearly, I just couldn't bring myself to accept him as a replacement for my real father.

It seemed that my mother's newfound love for her new life intensified her disdain for her old one, which included me. She wanted to erase all traces of her past, and I reminded her of a time she wanted to forget. It was a bitter pill to swallow, realizing that I no longer held a place in her heart.

As I looked at the man who was now my stepfather, I couldn't help but feel we were both about to get caught in crossfire. I knew I couldn't stay in a place where I was no longer wanted, but I also couldn't bear the thought of leaving my father behind.

Little did I know that the events that followed would lead me on a journey of self-discovery and transformation, a quest to become the fearless individual I had always admired in my father. The divorce was just the beginning of my story, a story that would be marked by challenges, adventures, and a relentless pursuit of fearlessness.

In the midst of my parents' chaotic divorce, I clung fiercely to one truth: my loyalty to my biological father. He was my rock, the unwavering presence in my life, and I refused to let that bond crumble. The mere thought of living in Baltimore, separated from my dad, filled me with a stubborn determination to resist my mother's wishes.

One summer, as my 13th birthday approached, my mother seemed to sense my growing unhappiness. Perhaps it was the way I gazed longingly at the old photos of my father and me, or maybe she finally understood the depth of my loyalty. Whatever the reason, she made a surprising decision. She allowed me to visit my father for the summer. At the time, I didn't fully grasp the significance of this gesture. I was just thrilled at the prospect of spending time with my dad, my hero. I packed my bags with a sense of excitement, not realizing that this summer visit would become a defining moment in my life.

That summer was a bittersweet blend of laughter and tears. My father and I made the most of every moment, cherishing the simple pleasures of life. We went fishing at the nearby lake, played catch in the park, and stayed up late talking about our dreams. Those memories, now etched in my heart, took on an almost sacred quality.

CHAPTER 3

THE GREAT ESCAPE

The sun-drenched days of summer in Newark were a stark contrast to the cold, sterile courtroom where my parents battled for my custody. The determination that had fueled my mom's career and my dad's fearlessness now clashed in a high-stakes showdown.

As I sat there, a 13-year-old caught in the middle of their fierce rivalry, the weight of their discord pressed down on me. Their once-happy marriage had soured into a ceaseless feud. What was supposed to be my childhood became an endless cycle of arguments, angry phone calls, and bitter exchanges.

My dad's house, the first floor of a multi-unit property he had inherited from my grandfather, was my sanctuary. Here, I had grown up amid tales of rebellion and stories of fearlessness. My dad had nurtured in me a spirit that refused to be broken. No matter how hard life hit, he taught me to hit back harder.

My mom's move to Baltimore, fueled by her ambition and career aspirations, had marked the beginning of a physical separation between my parents. The geographical distance created an emotional chasm that grew wider with each passing day. But what truly intensified the turmoil was her remarriage. She had urged me to call her new husband "dad," a demand that seemed to erase everything my real dad had meant to me. My mom's newfound love for her new life had a dark flip side—an intensified hatred for her old one, and I was a part of that old life she wanted to erase.

In those days, I was stuck between two worlds. My father, my hero, and my mother, whom I loved dearly but no longer recognized. I felt like an unwilling pawn in their bitter game of divorce. My dad's determination to keep me with him mirrored my own. We weren't just father and son; we were a team against the odds.

CHAPTER 4

CAUGHT BETWEEN TWO WORLDS

Hours later, as the sun cast long shadows across the courthouse steps, I found myself sitting on the stone ledge, my father beside me. The judge had granted us a few precious hours together before I had to reluctantly return to Baltimore with my mother. It was a temporary respite, a brief oasis of happiness in the midst of a bitter custody battle.

My father and I clung to every moment, knowing that our time together was slipping away like grains of sand through our fingers. We laughed, talked, and even shared an ice cream cone from the nearby vendor. But the looming reality hung over us like a dark cloud, and we couldn't ignore it for long.

As the agreed-upon deadline approached, I felt a familiar knot of dread in the pit of my stomach. Soon, the police officers would arrive to enforce the court order, and my father's comforting presence would be forcibly taken away from me. I couldn't let that happen again. Not this time.
The minutes ticked by, each second bringing us closer to the inevitable. My father's eyes met mine, and I could see the pain and determination in them. We both knew what had to be done. We had to make another daring escape, and this time, we were prepared.

The police officers arrived in their patrol cars, their badges glistening in the harsh sunlight. The lead officer, a stern-faced woman named Officer Ramirez, approached us. "Ernie, it's time to go with your mom," she said, her voice lacking the sympathy that even Officer Jenkins had tried to convey earlier.

My father, never one to back down, stood up and faced the officer. "We need more time," he implored. "Just a few more hours. Please, let him stay."

Officer Ramirez shook her head. "I'm sorry, but the court order is clear. It's time."

But my father was not one to give up easily. He glanced at me, a silent understanding passing between us. I nodded, my heart pounding with a mix of fear and determination. We had a plan, and we were going to execute it flawlessly.

As Officer Ramirez reached out to take my hand, I bolted from the steps and ran as fast as my little legs could carry me. It was a daring escape, just like in the movies, and I was on my own. My father stayed behind, facing the officers with a steely resolve, ready to buy me the time I needed. I darted through the bustling crowd, dodging pedestrians and slipping between parked cars. My heart raced, but I knew I couldn't stop. I had to make it to the predetermined spot, where my father's friend, LaDeeDa, would be waiting with a getaway car. It was a race against time, and my determination was unwavering. The streets blurred past me as I sprinted, my breath coming in ragged gasps. I could hear the distant shouts of the police officers behind me, but I couldn't afford to look back. I had to keep going, keep running, keep fighting.

Finally, I spotted LaDeeDa's car up ahead. It was a beacon of hope, and I pushed myself harder, my legs burning with effort. As I reached the car, I leaped into the waiting vehicle, breathless but exhilarated. LaDeeDa wasted no time, flooring the gas pedal, and we sped away from the chaos behind us.
The police officers, left in our dust, were no match for a determined kid and a fast car. I glanced out of the rear window, watching as they grew smaller and smaller in the distance. We had done it. I had escaped their clutches once again. Back at my father's place, a mix of emotions overwhelmed me. Relief, triumph, and a sense of belonging filled the room. My dad hugged me tightly, and I knew that no matter what happened next, we were a team, and we weren't going down without a fight.

The news of my daring escape quickly reached the judge's ears. The courtroom, now seemingly far away, would have to acknowledge one undeniable truth: I wanted to be with my dad more than anything in the world. My father had demonstrated his unwavering determination to be in my life, even if it meant defying the court's orders. The judge had no choice but to reconsider her decision. A wave of relief washed over me, and tears of joy filled my eyes. I couldn't believe it. We had won. My father had fought for me, and he had won.

The journey had been long and arduous, filled with challenges and obstacles that had tested our resolve. But in the end, it was our determination, our unbreakable bond, and our daring escape that had secured our victory.

CHAPTER 5

THE FATEFUL DAY OF THE FIRE

In the heart of Newark, New Jersey, my father and I witnessed the culmination of a hard-fought courtroom battle. It was a battle that had granted me the precious gift of living with my father, a victory that filled my young heart with unparalleled joy. Newark became our new home, a place where life was a daily hustle, and we cherished the little moments.

My father, a hardworking man, labored tirelessly to keep food on the table and a roof over our heads. His dedication was unwavering, his love immeasurable. I basked in the glow of our newfound life, the sense of belonging, and the comfort of being with the parent I had missed dearly.

But as the days turned into weeks, the initial euphoria began to fade, replaced by a lesson I would carry with me forever: that victories often came hand in hand with consequences.
On a day like any other, a typical day filled with hope and promise, tragedy struck. Our house, the place we called home, was reduced to smoldering ruins. The catalyst for this disaster had been a simple mistake, an innocent mishap that would change our lives forever. The air in the small, dimly lit kitchen was thick with tension, and the pungent aroma of simmering chicken wafted through the room. I stood in front of the stove, a sense of unease settling over me as I watched the sizzling chicken breasts in the pan. It was the fateful day that would forever be etched in my memory—the day of the accidental fire. And this wasn't just any house; it was my grandfather's house, passed down to my dad after my grandfather's death right before my birth, and now the place I called home after running away from my mother's oppressive grasp.

My life had been a relentless battleground, a constant struggle to break free from my mother's oppressive grip. The weight of choosing my father over her had pushed me to the brink, and I was desperately seeking a moment of respite.

My friend, Bobo, sat on the couch in the adjacent living room, his eyes fixed on the television screen as we played Madden. It was a feeble attempt to escape the suffocating atmosphere that had become my life. The virtual football game provided a fleeting distraction, a brief respite from the turmoil that raged within me.

As I stared at the chicken in the pan, I couldn't help but feel overwhelmed. The pressure was mounting, and the emotional burden on my shoulders felt almost unbearable. I had been dealing with the aftermath of my parents' custody battle, a traumatic experience that had left me feeling like a pawn in their never-ending war. My father had lost the battle in the courtroom, and now I was living with him in my grandmother's house.

The house itself was a relic of the past, filled with memories of my grandfather that I would never get to share. Its creaky floorboards and faded wallpaper held stories of a bygone era, a time when my family was whole and happy.

I glanced at the clock on the kitchen wall, realizing that I had left the chicken unattended for too long. The guilt that had been gnawing at me intensified. The pressure of my circumstances and the overwhelming guilt I felt for choosing my father over my mother had caused me to momentarily lose focus.

I rushed back to the stove, turning off the burner and grabbing a towel to handle the hot pan. But it was too late. Smoke billowed from the pan, and I could see the flames licking at the edges of the dishtowel. Panic surged through me as I desperately tried to smother the fire, but it had already gained a foothold.

"Bobo!" I shouted, my voice quivering with fear and urgency. But Bobo, as soon as he saw the fire, ran in fear, disappearing out of the house.

Without help, I had to confront the blazing inferno alone. I grabbed a nearby fire extinguisher and when I detached the hose from its assembly it disintegrated from never being used and it went beyond expiration. Since the out of service fire extinguisher would be no match for this blazing fire I retreated.

I rushed outside, gasping for breath, to see my grandmother approaching, her eyes filled with worry. When she saw the smoldering ruins of her beloved home, she let out a horrified gasp and nearly fainted. My heart sank as I witnessed the pain and anguish in her eyes.
The accidental fire was a tragic consequence of the emotional turmoil and inner conflict that had been my constant companions for years. It marked a turning point in my life, prompting me to embark on a journey of redemption and self-discovery, all while trying to make amends for the destruction I had caused in the home that held so many precious memories.

CHAPTER 6

THE BEGINNING OF A JOURNEY

In the aftermath of the devastating fire that had consumed my father's house, my life had taken an unexpected turn. The charred remains of our once-beloved home served as a stark reminder of the mistakes and lapses that had led to that fateful day. My father and I found ourselves in a relentless cycle of moving from house to house, shelter to shelter, in search of stability.

Despite the chaos that had become our daily existence, a glimmer of determination flickered within me. The fire had taken away our physical home, but it hadn't extinguished my will to rise above my past mistakes. I knew that dwelling on guilt and regret would lead nowhere, and I needed to take control of my destiny.

My father, though worn down by the custody battle and the subsequent upheaval, remained a steadfast source of support. His love was a beacon of hope in our tumultuous lives, and I was determined to rebuild the fractured bond between us. We shared a common pain and a common goal – to heal and move forward together.

Rebuilding our relationship wasn't easy. Words often failed to convey the depth of our emotions, but in those moments of shared silence, we found a connection that transcended language. Like a wounded animal finding its way back to trust, we began to mend.

The years passed, marked by our transient lifestyle, but also by the slow but steady healing of old wounds. The guilt and shame that had once consumed me began to lose their grip. It was as if the fire had purged not only our physical home but also the emotional baggage I had carried for so long.

The unwavering presence of my father and the few friends we made along the way, though fleeting, provided a sense of stability in our otherwise tumultuous lives. While I never saw Bobo again after that fateful day of the fire, the memory of his friendship remained a bittersweet reminder of the past.

It wasn't until we reached our third shelter that the city's assistance program stepped in to help my family find stable housing. The prospect of a permanent home brought a glimmer of hope we hadn't felt in years. It was a chance to break free from the cycle of transience and finally establish some roots.

With each new shelter we called home and every step toward stability, I felt a growing sense of responsibility. The fire had taken away our physical home, but it had ignited a new sense of purpose within me. I realized that my journey was not just about personal redemption; it was about being a beacon of hope for others facing adversity.

As we finally found a stable place to call home, I knew that my journey was far from over. The road ahead would be challenging, but I was prepared. The fire had been a turning point, a moment when my lapse in focus had led to unintentional destruction, but it had also been a catalyst for change.

With unwavering determination, I stepped into the unknown, ready to heal the wounds of my past and make amends for the accidental fire that had forever altered the course of my life. My journey was a testament to the resilience of the human spirit, a journey of redemption and self-discovery that had only just begun.

CHAPTER 7

OFF THE BEATEN PATH

At the age of 18, my life was a promising tapestry of potential. I was young, full of energy, and itching for adventure. Football and boxing were my outlets, my ways of channeling the relentless aggression that coursed through my veins like an unstoppable river. It was clear to me that college was the path society expected me to take, the path they had shoved down my throat since I could remember. But as it turns out, life had other plans for me, ones far more twisted and exciting.

So, I dropped out and decided to chase a different dream. I became an EMT, a decision that shocked my family and friends. Even as an EMT, I couldn't quite escape the gravitational pull of my past. My old man had always warned me about the dangers of my neighborhood friends, but I was a stubborn, impressionable young man who had to learn things the hard way. My friends from the neighborhood still hung around, their magnetic allure impossible to resist. They'd pull me into late-night gatherings, sneaking a few beers in a dimly lit alley, and regaling me with tales of their escapades. It was exhilarating, a taste of the life I'd never known while growing up in the suffocating shadow of my mother's religious fervor.

But I was about to find out why my old man had warned me against these friendships. It was a sweltering summer night when I found myself driving through the city with my buddies, music blaring from the speakers, and the promise of adventure hanging in the air like an electric charge. We were cruising down a dimly lit street, the city's pulsating energy alive and intoxicating.
And then, without warning, the world tilted on its axis.Cops. Flashing sirens. In the rearview mirror.

Panic seized me, and my heart pounded like a drum in a heavy metal band. My buddies, oblivious to the impending storm, continued to laugh and joke, completely unaware of the danger lurking behind us. I cursed myself for being so reckless, for allowing my longing for excitement to cloud my judgment.

As the police cruiser pulled us over, I couldn't help but notice the wicked irony in the situation. Here I was, a young man who had tried to break free from the constraints of society's expectations, now facing the cold, unforgiving reality of the law. Dark humor, they say, is the best kind of humor, and in that moment, I found it hard not to laugh at the absurdity of it all.
The officer approached the car, his flashlight cutting through the darkness like a searchlight seeking out our sins. My buddies, who had been so carefree just moments ago, suddenly adopted the demeanor of choirboys caught red-handed with a stolen cookie. It was as if the weight of the world had descended upon us.

The officer, a burly man with a stern expression, eyed each of us with suspicion. He asked the usual questions – license, registration, and all that jazz. I did my best to stay composed, but my hands trembled as I fumbled for my wallet. I couldn't afford to get into trouble, not now, not when I had just started down a different path in life.

But as I handed over my ID, I couldn't shake the nagging feeling that something was about to go terribly wrong. The officer's eyes lingered on my face a little too long, and then he muttered something into his radio. Within minutes, more police cars arrived at the scene, their sirens wailing like a chorus of banshees.

They ordered us out of the car, handcuffed us, and began searching the vehicle. My buddies and I exchanged nervous glances, our laughter replaced by a heavy silence. It felt like a nightmare, a surreal descent into a world where the rules had been rewritten, and we were the unwitting pawns.

As they searched the car, one of the officers found a small baggie tucked away under the seat. It contained an illegal substance and it did not belong to me, it was enough to send a chill down my spine. They arrested us on the spot, handcuffs digging into our wrists like a painful reminder of our newfound predicament.

I couldn't believe it. I was being wrongfully charged with a crime I did not commit. It was a cruel twist of fate, a stark reminder of the systemic injustices that plagued my neighborhood – a place where racial profiling and mass incarceration were big business.

As they drove us away in the back of a squad car, I couldn't help but wonder how I had ended up in this nightmare. Life had taken an unexpected detour, one that would test my resolve and push me to my limits. I had no idea what lay ahead, but one thing was certain – the path had just taken a dark and dangerous turn.

CHAPTER 8

THE TERRIFYING NIGHT

The police cruiser cut through the darkness, its tires humming on the asphalt as it carried me away from the scene of my wrongful arrest. The flashing red and blue lights cast eerie patterns on the backseat's hard, unforgiving surface. My hands, still cuffed, rested heavily in my lap, serving as a grim reminder of the nightmare I had just experienced.

As the city streets passed by, my thoughts raced faster than the car. Fear, confusion, and helplessness gnawed at the edges of my mind, threatening to consume me whole. I felt like a passenger in my own life, a spectator to the events unfolding around me.

The brutality of the arrest was a fresh wound, a raw and searing pain that pulsed with every beat of my heart. My body bore the physical scars of the encounter, but it was the emotional scars that cut the deepest. I couldn't shake the anger, the frustration, the disbelief that had taken root in my soul.

I knew, beyond a shadow of a doubt, that I had been racially profiled. It was an injustice so blatant, so cruel, that it felt like a punch to the gut. The officers who had arrested me didn't care about the truth; they only saw the color of my skin and assumed my guilt.

In the back of that police car, I was alone with my thoughts, my mind a whirlwind of emotions. Anger burned within me like a fire, a fierce and unrelenting rage at the injustice of it all. How could this happen? How could those sworn to protect us be the ones inflicting harm?

Frustration welled up inside me, a torrent of helplessness that threatened to drown me. I wanted to fight back, to shout my innocence from the rooftops, but I knew that it would only make things worse. The system was stacked against people like me, and speaking out often led to even harsher consequences.

But it was the disbelief that cut the deepest. How could I go from

laughing and joking with my friends to sitting in the back of a police car, falsely accused and brutally arrested? The world had shifted beneath my feet, and I felt like I was tumbling into an abyss of injustice.
Time lost its meaning as the cruiser carried me further away from the familiar streets of my neighborhood. Minutes felt like hours, and hours felt like days. I had been separated from my friends, who had been released after only a few hours of processing, while I remained trapped in this metal cage.

Eventually, the police car pulled up to the imposing edifice of the county jail. The building loomed in the night like a fortress of despair, its cold, concrete walls a stark contrast to the warm summer air outside. I was led out of the car and into the belly of the beast, my steps heavy with the weight of my predicament.
The jailhouse was a place of harsh realities and unyielding rules. It was a world unto itself, governed by a code I had yet to decipher. I was subjected to the dehumanizing process of intake —fingerprinting, mugshots, and interrogations that felt more like interrogations.

Hours turned into days, and days into weeks as I languished behind bars. I felt like a forgotten soul in a world that had moved on without me. My friends, who had once been my source of adventure and laughter, were out there somewhere, living their lives while I remained trapped in this bleak existence.

The emotional turmoil of those days was relentless. I missed my friends, my family, and the simple joys of life that I had taken for granted. Anger simmered just below the surface, a constant reminder of the injustice that had been done to me.

But it was the disappointment in my father's voice that haunted me the most. He had warned me, time and time again, about the dangers of the crowd I ran with. He had cautioned me against making choices that could lead to a dead-end like this. And now, here I was, paying the price for my stubbornness and naivety.

The memory of that morning when he made me walk home from the jailhouse was a bitter pill to swallow. It was a long, solitary journey of shame and regret, a stark reminder of the consequences of my choices. I felt the weight of his disappointment with every step, and it was a burden that would stay with me long after my release.

My friends, oblivious to the brutality and injustice I had endured, wanted me to continue hanging out with them. They didn't understand the depths of my father's disappointment, the pain that had been etched into my soul. But I couldn't bear the thought of seeing my father that upset again. I had let him down in the worst way possible, and I never wanted to see that look of disappointment on his face ever again. They will always be my friends. I just had to learn the tough lesson that some journeys must be traveled alone.

As I turned my back on the crowd that had once been my source of adventure, I knew that my path had taken a dark and unexpected turn. That episode had been terrifying, but it had also been a harsh wake-up call. It was time to reevaluate my choices, to find a new way forward in a world that seemed determined to hold me back.

CHAPTER 9

THE STAIN OF A FELONY CONVICTION

The weight of a potential felony conviction hung over me like a dark cloud, casting a long and menacing shadow on my future. It was a stain that threatened to seep into every aspect of my life, like an indelible mark that would forever define me. The gravity of the situation was overwhelming, and as I sat in that dimly lit jail cell, I couldn't help but confront the harsh reality that lay ahead.

A felony conviction was no ordinary stain on one's record; it was a scarlet letter that branded you for life. It meant limited opportunities, closed doors, and a constant battle to prove oneself to a world that had already judged you. I knew that even if I managed to escape this nightmare unscathed, the mark on my record would always be a reminder of the injustice I had endured.
The potential consequences weighed heavily on my mind. Employment opportunities would be scarce, if not non-existent. Many doors would slam shut before I even had a chance to knock. The world was quick to judge, and a felony conviction was a scarlet letter that couldn't be hidden or erased.

As the days turned into weeks, I found myself at a crossroads. The decision that loomed before me was a grim one, a choice that no one should ever have to make. I could plead guilty, accept a lesser sentence, and carry the stain of a felony conviction for the rest of my life. Or I could fight, roll the dice in a system that had already proven itself to be stacked against me, and hope for a miracle.

It was a decision that felt like a noose tightening around my neck. I was trapped in a Kafkaesque nightmare, caught in the gears of a system that ground people like me into dust. And yet, I couldn't simply surrender to the darkness. The injustice I had suffered fueled a fire within me, a burning determination to prove my innocence and escape the clutches of this nightmare.
But I quickly learned that the pursuit of justice was a treacherous path, one fraught with pitfalls and obstacles at every turn. My court-appointed lawyer, a man more concerned with the creases in his expensive suit than the intricacies of my case, provided little

comfort or guidance. It was clear that I would have to take matters into my own hands if I wanted to stand a chance.
I made a fateful decision that would alter the course of my life. I chose to join the Navy, not out of a sense of duty or patriotism, but out of a desperate hope that it might sway the judgment of a future judge. Perhaps, I thought to myself, a judge would be less inclined to send a young man brave enough to fight for his country to prison.

The Navy became my lifeline, my ticket to a future untainted by the stain of a felony conviction. I threw myself into the rigorous training, determined to excel in every way possible. It wasn't easy, and the path was filled with challenges, but I clung to the belief that this sacrifice would be worth it in the end.
The days turned into months as I trained relentlessly, my focus unwavering. I pushed myself to the limits, both physically and mentally, knowing that the opportunity for a fresh start lay at the end of this grueling journey. I couldn't allow myself to falter; I had too much to lose.

The Navy provided a sense of purpose, a chance to prove myself beyond the confines of a courtroom. It offered a glimpse of a future where the stain of a felony conviction might not define me, where I could escape the shadows of that terrifying night.

But it wasn't just about personal redemption. I wanted to show the world that I could rise above the injustice that had been done to me. I wanted to be a beacon of hope for others who had been wronged by a system that seemed stacked against them. I wanted to prove that the human spirit could endure even the darkest of nights and emerge stronger on the other side.

As I continued to train and prepare for my future in the Navy, I knew that the road ahead would be challenging. The stain of a felony conviction would always be a part of my story, a reminder of the injustice I had faced. But I refused to let it define me. I was determined to rise above it, to prove that I was more than the sum of my past mistakes.

And so, with each grueling day of training, with each obstacle I overcame, I inched closer to a future where the darkness of that terrifying night would be nothing more than a distant memory. My determination burned brighter than ever, a beacon of hope in the darkest of times, and I was ready to face whatever challenges lay ahead on my path to redemption.

CHAPTER 10

UNFORESEEN BLESSINGS

The Navy. It was a path I had chosen out of desperation, a way to escape the looming specter of a felony conviction that threatened to stain my life forever. But as I stepped onto the rigid, orderly world of military life, I couldn't help but feel a pang of nostalgia for the freedom I had sacrificed.

The Navy offered unexpected blessings, though, that I couldn't have anticipated. It brought structure, discipline, and personal growth into my life, like rays of light piercing the darkness. In a twisted turn of events, I found myself thriving in a world that had once seemed so foreign and uninviting.

I'll be honest; my initial reluctance was palpable. The strict routines, the rigid hierarchy, the countless rules and regulations—it all felt like a far cry from the carefree days I had left behind. I longed for the freedom to do as I pleased, to chart my own course without being beholden to authority.

But beneath that initial resistance lay a burning motivation—a fire fueled by my aversion to authority and a deep-seated desire to prove myself. I had never been one to bow down to those who sought to control me, and the Navy was no exception. I was determined to carve out my own path, to show that I could rise above my past and excel in this new, structured environment.

The Navy provided me with a sense of purpose that I hadn't known before. It gave me a mission, a reason to push myself beyond my limits. The discipline it demanded was harsh, but it was also liberating in its own way. It was a structure that I could rely on, a framework that gave my life meaning.

My aversion to authority, though, remained a constant driving force. I refused to be just another face in the crowd, just another cog in the military machine. I wanted to stand out, to prove that I could excel in spite of the rules and regulations that sought to constrain me.

And excel I did. I took every opportunity to showcase my skills and determination, earning the respect of my peers and superiors alike. I embraced the Navy's core values—honor, courage, and commitment—and made them my own. It was a way to prove that I was more than the sum of my past mistakes, more than the stain of a felony conviction.

The Navy also brought unexpected friendships into my life—bonds forged in the crucible of shared challenges and triumphs. My fellow sailors became my brothers and sisters, a support network that I hadn't known I needed. They understood the struggles I had faced, and they saw the potential in me that others had overlooked.

As I settled into this new chapter of my life, I couldn't help but reflect on the unforeseen blessings that had come my way. The Navy had given me structure and discipline, personal growth and a sense of purpose. It had brought unexpected friendships and a chance to prove myself on my own terms.

As I looked ahead to the challenges that lay on the horizon, I knew that the Navy had brought unexpected blessings into my life. It had given me the tools and the opportunity to redefine myself, to escape the dark cloud of my past and emerge stronger, more determined, and more motivated than ever before.

CHAPTER 11

COUNTDOWN TO DISCHARGE

As the days dwindled down to the final stretch of my Navy service, a strange mixture of emotions churned within me. I counted down the hours, minutes, and seconds to my honorable discharge, all while maintaining an unwavering focus on the imminent goal that had propelled me through this chapter of my life.

The allure of freedom was undeniable, a siren's song that beckoned me with promises of unrestricted choices and unbridled adventure. But despite the tantalizing whispers of liberty, I remained steadfast in my dedication to my duties.

The military had instilled in me a set of virtues that had become my guiding principles—leadership, honor, and commitment. These values were not mere words; they were the bedrock upon which I had built my character and actions.

The rapid ascent through the Navy ranks had been unexpected, but it was a testament to my unwavering determination and the virtues instilled in me by the military. I had seized every opportunity to showcase my skills and leadership abilities, and it had paid off in ways I had never imagined.

I had seen the world through the eyes of a sailor, from the vast, open seas to the foreign shores that beckoned with their mysteries and wonders. I had stood on the decks of naval vessels, my chest swelling with pride as I saluted the flag that represented the ideals I held dear. I had faced challenges that tested my limits and pushed me to exceed them, and I had emerged stronger and more resilient.

But it wasn't just the physical challenges that had shaped me; it was the moral and ethical principles instilled in me by the military. Leadership meant more than giving orders; it meant leading by example and earning the respect of those you led. Honor was not just a word; it was a code of conduct that dictated every action and decision. Commitment was a lifelong pledge to uphold the values I had come to cherish.

The recognition I had received for my exceptional performance in the Navy was not just a source of pride; it was a validation of the person I had become. I had proven that a young man with a felony conviction could overcome the odds and excel in a world that had once seemed closed off to him.

I knew that the allure of freedom would always be there, but I was no longer the young man I had once been. I was a sailor who had earned the respect of his peers and superiors, a leader who had proven himself in the face of challenges, and a person who had learned that true success was measured not in wealth, but in the impact one had on the world and the people around them.

CHAPTER 12

THE CROSSROADS

The moment of decision loomed before me like a fork in the road, each path leading to a vastly different future. As I neared my honorable discharge from the Navy, the chain of command saw potential within me, urging me to make a career within the organization. It was a tempting proposition, one that offered stability, respect, and a life within the structured confines of military service.

But within the recesses of my mind, a battle raged—a conflict born from competing desires. On one hand, there was the allure of a Navy career, the promise of a steady paycheck and the camaraderie of my fellow sailors. On the other, there was personal success and financial independence, a path that whispered of untapped potential and uncharted horizons.

I was torn between these two worlds, each vying for my allegiance. The chain of command saw something in me that I had come to see in myself—a leader, a problem-solver, and a disciplined sailor. They believed that my future was within the Navy, and they made their case with a persuasive mix of encouragement and recognition.

But I couldn't shake the burning ambition that smoldered within me. It was a fire that had been kindled during my time in the Navy, a desire to become an asset to myself, to carve out a destiny of my own making. The virtues instilled in me—leadership, honor, and commitment—had become my guiding principles, shaping the decisions I made and the person I had become.

As I grappled with this internal struggle, I couldn't help but reflect on the lessons I had learned and the person I had become during my time in the Navy. I had been given a rare opportunity—to redefine myself, to rise above the constraints of my past, and to become a force for good in the world.

The burning ambition within me was a powerful force, one that drove me to seek personal success and financial independence. I wanted to prove to myself and to the world that I could excel on my own terms, that I could create a life that was a testament to my determination and resolve.

But I also knew that success, in its truest sense, was not measured solely in financial gain. It was measured in the impact one had on the world and the people around them. The virtues I had acquired in the Navy were not just words on a page; they were a code of conduct that dictated every action and decision.

As I stood at the crossroads of my future, I knew that the decision I made would shape the trajectory of my life. It was a choice that carried weight and consequence, and I couldn't afford to make it lightly. I had a burning desire to utilize the virtues I had acquired in the Navy to inspire others and create a lasting impact beyond the military.

And so, as I faced the chain of command and their persuasive arguments for a Navy career, I knew that I had already made my choice. The allure of personal success and financial independence beckoned to me with promises of uncharted horizons, and I was determined to seize that opportunity.

I knew that the road ahead would be challenging, filled with uncertainties and obstacles. But I was no stranger to challenges, and I had learned that true success was not measured solely in material gain, but in the impact one had on the world and the people around them.

As I prepared to embark on a different path, one that would lead me away from the structured confines of the Navy, I carried with me the virtues of leadership, honor, and commitment that had become a part of my identity. They were the compass that would guide my actions and decisions, and I was determined to create a life that was a testament to their enduring influence.

The crossroads had come and gone, and I had chosen my path

—a path that promised personal success, financial independence, and the opportunity to inspire others. As I looked ahead to the challenges and adventures that lay in wait, I knew that I was ready to chart my own destiny and leave a lasting impact on the world.

PART 2

WALL STREET ODYSSEY

CHAPTER 13

THE AUDACIOUS DREAM

In the sprawling heart of New York City, where ambition and dreams were currency, I, Ernie G, a freshly discharged Navy veteran, found myself at the crossroads of a new journey—an audacious dream to become a stockbroker on the famed Wall Street.

The streets of Manhattan teemed with frenetic energy, mirroring the fervor that coursed through my veins. My determination was relentless, and my ambition blazed like the city's dazzling lights. I had stared down the most formidable challenges during my time in the Navy, and now, I was determined to conquer the world of high finance.

In the heart of the bustling financial epicenter that is Wall Street, dreams have been known to materialize into reality. For Ernie, this realization was both a challenge and an irresistible allure. He understood that within the labyrinthine corridors of the financial world, the elite were the masters of their destinies, orchestrating the grand symphony of wealth and influence. Money, as he discerned, was the currency of power that greased the wheels of the world. Ernie envisioned himself among the privileged few, yearning for the Rolls Royces, private jets, and penthouse suites with a doorman's nod of recognition. His dreams sparkled with diamonds and the kind of watches that whispered affluence with every tick. As he looked forward to an unknown future, he sensed a mysterious presence, a partner yet to reveal herself, someone who would share in his aspirations for a life that gleamed with opulence and extravagance, their destinies intertwined by fate, yet shrouded in enigmatic anticipation. Ernie was a true romantic deep down inside and really wanted to break social norms and make it cool to be the leader of a traditional nuclear family.

But beneath the surface of my dreams lay the looming shadows of my past mistakes. A felony conviction, a stubborn stain on my record, cast a pall over my aspirations. The audacious dream that beckoned me was marred by the harsh reality of my history.

Yet, I knew that the key to unlocking the gates of Wall Street was the coveted Series 7 license. It was a testament to one's knowledge and expertise, a pass to the inner sanctum of finance. Despite the conviction on my record, I was determined to obtain it, to prove that my past did not define my future.

The classroom where I prepared for the Series 7 exam was a haven for seekers of financial wisdom, each one chasing their own version of the American Dream. The instructor's voice was a constant hum, dissecting the intricacies of the financial world. But amid the lectures and textbooks, my thoughts often strayed to the choices that had led me to this point.

The Series 7 license was more than just a piece of paper; it was a ticket to the grand theater of finance. The knowledge required to obtain it was vast and complex, but my resolve was unwavering. I devoured textbooks, immersed myself in financial reports, and dissected market trends. Each day was a step closer to my goal, a step further from the shadows of my past.
The virtues instilled in me by the Navy—leadership, honor, commitment—became my guiding stars. They whispered that true success was not defined solely by material wealth but by the impact one had on the world and its people.

With unyielding determination, I embarked on a different path—one that led me away from the structured confines of corporate life. The world of finance was a tumultuous sea, a place where only the boldest navigators thrived. I would rely on the virtues instilled within me to navigate these uncharted waters.

But before I could take the Series 7 exam, I faced an unexpected hurdle. In order to have the chance to take the test, I had to agree to a year-long internship, a grueling trial by fire. The pay was a mere pittance, a paltry $500 per month, far below minimum wage. It was a stark reminder that the path to redemption was not paved with gold but with determination and sacrifice.

CHAPTER 14

UNWAVERING OPTIMISM

In the concrete jungle of Wall Street, where towering skyscrapers cast long shadows over dreams and ambitions, I found myself in a peculiar situation—an interview with Tiny, the second-in-command of Carmine's firm. Tiny was anything but tiny; he stood at a towering height of six feet four inches and tipped the scales at a staggering 500 pounds. The irony of his name was not lost on anyone who met him, but perhaps it was a testament to his larger-than-life presence in the world of finance.

As I walked into his office, a knot of nervousness twisted in my gut. My criminal record loomed like a dark cloud, an unwelcome specter that could shatter my dreams of becoming a stockbroker on Wall Street. Yet, Tiny, a man of imposing stature, had a soft spot for veterans, and I hoped that my military service would earn me some leniency.

Tiny's eyes, hidden behind a pair of thick glasses, bore into me as he reviewed my application. His massive frame seemed to fill the room, making the office feel more like a closet. I cleared my throat, trying to steady my nerves, and began explaining my past and my conviction.

To my surprise, Tiny listened attentively, his expression unreadable. When I finished, he leaned back in his oversized leather chair and let out a deep sigh. "You've got guts, kid," he rumbled, his voice surprisingly gentle for a man of his size. "Most people would've tried to hide that conviction, but you came clean. I respect that."

His words were like a lifeline, and I felt a glimmer of hope. It turned out that Tiny had a nephew who had served in the military, and he held veterans in high regard. With his nod of approval, my chances of making it onto Wall Street felt a little less remote.

In the early days of my Wall Street journey, optimism and hope coursed through my veins. I embraced the challenge with unwavering determination, knowing that this was my chance at redemption. I had to prove not only to Tiny but also to myself that I could succeed in this cutthroat world.

My routine was rigorous—I had to be the first one in the office and the last one to leave. The world of finance was a relentless beast, and I was determined to master its intricacies. I devoured financial reports, analyzed market trends, and absorbed knowledge like a sponge. Each day brought new challenges, and I met them head-on with the resilience born of a life filled with hardship.

I was warned about the senior brokers—the veterans of Wall Street who took pleasure in making newcomers' lives miserable. But they had no inkling of the battles I had fought in the past, and their attempts to cause me discomfort were nothing more than pure amusement. To me, their antics were like child's play, and I found their feeble attempts at intimidation to be nothing but a source of entertainment.

This resilience, this iron will, did not go unnoticed. Carmine, the boss of the firm, appreciated my unyielding determination and my ability to weather the storm of Wall Street with a grin. In a world where he often saw his employees as weak, sensitive, and fragile, I was a breath of fresh air.

Carmine believed in the survival of the fittest, and he saw in me a kindred spirit. He knew that I had faced hardships that most of his employees couldn't even fathom, and he respected me for it. My unwavering optimism and my ability to rise above adversity made me an asset in his eyes, a stark contrast to the others who wilted under pressure.

As I navigated the high-stakes world of finance, I did so with a sense of purpose and a smile on my face. I had overcome insurmountable odds in the past, and I was determined to do the same on Wall Street. The audacious dream that had ignited within me was no longer a distant goal but a tangible reality, and I was ready to seize it with both hands.

CHAPTER 15

THE WALL STREET BULLY

In the heart of the financial district, where ambition flowed like a river and fortunes were won and lost with the blink of an eye, there stood a colossus named Carmine. He wasn't just the boss; he was the embodiment of success in the world of high finance. A towering figure, both in stature and influence, he was the kind of man who made you question your worth before your morning coffee had cooled.

Carmine had a way of sizing you up, of dissecting your character with a single glance. He had an uncanny knack for spotting weaknesses that most people didn't even know they possessed. And once he identified that chink in your armor, he'd exploit it, pushing you to your limits and beyond.

His first piece of advice to me was simple yet profound: "Read 'Rhinoceros Success.' It's the first book I was told to read when I was in your spot." Carmine had mastered the book, and in many ways, he was the rhino of its pages personified. The book's message was clear—to charge forward with unwavering determination, to be relentless in the pursuit of one's goals. Carmine embodied that ethos to the core.

His breakfast meetings were legendary, and they were not for the faint of heart. It was as if he had a talent for making you feel bad about yourself before the day had even begun. But Carmine believed in tough love, in pushing his proteges to their limits. He knew that success in the cutthroat world of finance required a thick skin and an unyielding spirit.

If Carmine spotted weakness in you—and he always did—he would do his best to extract it, to force you to confront your vulnerabilities head-on. There was no room for fragility in his world, no tolerance for mediocrity. If he determined that your weaknesses were insurmountable, you were fired without hesitation.

The corporate culture that revolved around Carmine was both revered and feared. It was a world where excellence was the only currency that mattered, and failure was not an option. The mantra that echoed through the firm's halls was simple yet all-encompassing: "What would Carmine do?" It wasn't just a saying; it was a way of life. To succeed in his firm, you had to channel your inner Carmine, to think like him, act like him, and, most importantly, produce like him. Carmine had his favorites, and they were the living proof of his mentorship. Peanut and Billy were two such proteges, and their stories were the stuff of legends within the firm. Carmine seen something in them, something that he believed could be forged into greatness.

Under Carmine's unrelenting guidance, Peanut and Billy had flourished. They were now titans of Wall Street, cruising through the city in the latest Mercedes-Benz models and competing over who could flaunt the most expensive watch. Billy, the current champion of extravagance, had recently acquired a Philippe Patek Aquanaut—a timepiece so exquisite that it bordered on the absurd. It was a testament to the excesses of their success.

Carmine took immense pride in their achievements. He would regale us with stories of their journey, relishing his role as the mentor who had shaped their careers. His gruff exterior softened as he spoke about them, and a rare twinkle of genuine pride gleamed in his eyes. He wasn't just their boss; he was their mentor, and he reveled in that role.

But the world Carmine had built was not for the faint of heart. It was a world where only the strongest survived, where mediocrity was a cardinal sin, and where the pursuit of success was relentless. To thrive in his firm was to embrace the dark humor that permeated the world of finance, to find amusement in the absurdity of it all.

As I navigated this world under Carmine's watchful eye, I couldn't help but feel a sense of awe mixed with trepidation. He was a complex figure, a man who could inspire both fear and admiration. He had the ability to make you question your worth with a single glance, but he also had the power to make you believe that you could achieve greatness.

Carmine's expectations were sky-high, and his demands were unrelenting. He was a perfectionist, and he expected nothing less from those under his wing. He was a man who believed in the survival of the fittest, and he pushed us to our limits, testing our mettle and pushing us beyond what we thought were our boundaries.

Yet, there was a dark humor that permeated the world of finance, and Carmine embodied it perfectly. He found amusement in the absurdity of it all, in the cutthroat nature of Wall Street. He reveled in the chaos, in the thrill of the chase, and he expected us to do the same.
Carmine wasn't just a boss; he was a mentor, a guide through the treacherous terrain of Wall Street. He was a master of the game, a veteran who had weathered countless storms and emerged stronger each time. And he believed that if you could survive under his wing, you could thrive anywhere.

Carmine was a paradox—a man whose gruff exterior concealed a genuine desire to see his proteges succeed. He knew that not everyone could handle the pressure, the relentless pursuit of excellence. But for those who could, for those willing to endure the crucible of his leadership, the rewards were worth every sacrifice. Carmine was a boss like no other, and his legacy would live on in the traders and brokers who had dared to walk in his shadow.

CHAPTER 16

A MENTORSHIP BEGINS

Carmine, the imposing titan of Wall Street, had decided to take me under his wing, a decision that left me both exhilarated and anxious. He placed me in his top producing group, a group that had connections to the infamous Jordan Belfort, the "Wolf of Wall Street" before his fall from grace. It was as if I had been given a golden ticket to the heart of the financial kingdom, and I was determined to make the most of this opportunity.

My initial interactions with Carmine were nothing short of intimidating. He had a way of making you feel like a deer caught in the headlights, and it took every ounce of composure to maintain my cool. But beneath that gruff exterior, I sensed a genuine desire to see me succeed, and that gave me hope.

Carmine's mentorship was a unique blend of tough love and unwavering support. He pushed me to my limits, demanding nothing less than excellence. It was a mentorship dynamic reminiscent of the legendary boxing trainer Cus D'Amato and his protege Mike Tyson, a relationship built on trust, respect, and the relentless pursuit of greatness.

As I delved deeper into the world of finance under Carmine's guidance, I began to unravel the mysteries of wealth creation and market manipulation. It was a journey filled with revelations, each one bringing with it a profound sense of wisdom and insight. I learned to navigate the treacherous waters of Wall Street, to spot opportunities where others saw chaos, and to seize the moment with unyielding determination.

But with knowledge came a moral dilemma that weighed heavily on my conscience. The same insights that could be used to amass personal wealth could also be harnessed to benefit my community, to uplift those who had been left behind by the system. I found myself standing at a crossroads, torn between the allure of greed and the call of ethics, between the seductive power of wealth and the humility of service.

Carmine, with all his flaws and contradictions, became my guiding star in this moral quagmire. He had walked this path before me, and his lessons extended beyond the confines of finance. He taught me that true power lay not in the accumulation of riches, but in the impact one could have on the lives of others.

As I continued to learn from Carmine, I realized that his mentorship was not just about success in the world of finance; it was about becoming a better person. He challenged me to confront my weaknesses, to shed the layers of insecurity and doubt that had held me back for so long. He pushed me to be the best version of myself, both as a trader and as a human being.

Carmine was a man who had tasted the sweet nectar of success and had also known the bitter sting of failure. He had witnessed the darkest corners of the financial world and had emerged with his integrity intact. He showed me that it was possible to navigate the treacherous waters of Wall Street without losing one's soul, that it was possible to use one's knowledge and influence for the greater good.

Our interactions were peppered with moments of dark humor, as we navigated the absurdity of the financial world together. Carmine had a way of finding amusement in the chaos, in the cutthroat nature of our industry. He reminded me that, in the grand scheme of things, our pursuit of wealth and success was just a game—a high-stakes game, but a game nonetheless.

But it was a game that demanded our utmost dedication and focus. Carmine instilled in me a sense of discipline and commitment that went beyond anything I had ever known. He taught me to be the first in the office and the last person to leave, to be relentless in the pursuit of excellence. He believed that success was not a matter of chance but a matter of choice, and he expected nothing less than my absolute best.

As I continued to learn from Carmine, I couldn't help but be reminded of the words of Cus D'Amato to a young Mike Tyson: "The hero and the coward both feel the same fear, but it's what they do that makes them different." Carmine had the power to turn fear into fuel, to transform uncertainty into opportunity. He had a way of bringing out the hero in those willing to embrace the challenge.

But the journey was far from easy. It was a constant battle against self-doubt, against the allure of shortcuts and quick gains. Carmine reminded me that true success was built on a foundation of integrity and hard work, that there were no shortcuts to lasting greatness.

As the days turned into weeks and the weeks into months, I found myself caught in a whirlwind of growth and transformation. Carmine's mentorship was not just about acquiring knowledge; it was about becoming a person of character, a person who could navigate the complexities of the financial world with grace and integrity.

The struggle between greed and ethics, power and humility, continued to rage within me. But Carmine, with his unwavering support and guidance, showed me that it was possible to find a balance, to use the knowledge I had gained to make a positive impact on the world. He taught me that true success was not measured by the size of one's bank account but by the lives one could touch and the difference one could make.

CHAPTER 17

CARMINE'S REVELATION

The walls of Carmine's office seemed to close in on me as I sat across from him, the weight of his words bearing down on my chest like a ton of bricks. The world I had so meticulously built in my mind crumbled to pieces in an instant. It was a revelation that hit me like a sucker punch, stealing the very breath from my lungs.

"Ernie," Carmine began, his voice solemn and unwavering, "I've got some bad news. You can't become a stockbroker."

His words hung in the air, heavy with finality. I couldn't believe what I was hearing. All those hours, all those sacrifices, all those dreams I had woven around the idea of becoming a stockbroker—it had all been in vain. The felony conviction on my record was a towering wall that separated me from my aspirations.

I could feel my heart sink, and a crushing sense of devastation washed over me. It hurt so bad because I had sacrificed an entire year with the singular goal of becoming a broker in my mind. I had poured every ounce of my energy into this endeavor, and now it felt like it had all been for nothing.

But as I sat there, my dreams in tatters, Carmine's words began to penetrate the fog of my despair. "Ernie, life is a series of peaks and valleys," he said, his gaze unwavering. "We all make mistakes, and we all have our setbacks. But what separates the winners from the losers is how we deal with those setbacks. It's about turning mistakes into opportunities, about finding a new path when the old one is blocked."

Carmine's words were a revelation in themselves. He wasn't just delivering bad news; he was imparting a life lesson that extended far beyond the realm of finance. He was teaching me about resilience, about the ability to adapt and overcome, no matter the odds stacked against you.
As I grappled with his words, I realized that my journey with Carmine had never been just about becoming a stockbroker. It had

been about learning from a man who had seen the highs and lows of life, a man who had overcome his own setbacks and emerged stronger for it.

Carmine continued, "Ernie, I've seen countless young men and women come through these doors, full of dreams and ambitions. Some of them make it big, while others fall by the wayside. But the ones who succeed are the ones who don't let obstacles define them. They embrace the challenges, they learn from their mistakes, and they keep moving forward."

I nodded slowly, the weight of his words sinking in. Carmine wasn't just a mentor in finance; he was a mentor in life. He was teaching me that success wasn't a straight line but a winding path filled with twists and turns, and it was up to me to navigate it with courage and determination.

With each passing moment, the crushing disappointment I had initially felt began to transform into something else—resolve. I realized that my dreams of becoming a stockbroker weren't the only dreams worth pursuing. There were other avenues, other opportunities that lay before me, waiting to be explored.

Carmine's mentorship had taught me valuable lessons that extended beyond wealth accumulation. He had shown me the importance of integrity, of humility, and of using one's knowledge and influence for the greater good. He had reminded me that true success wasn't measured by the size of one's bank account but by the impact one could have on the lives of others.

With a newfound sense of purpose, I made a decision. I would embrace a new path to prosperity, one that transcended traditional measures of success. I would use my knowledge and wisdom to uplift my community, to effect positive change in the finance industry, and to prove that success could be defined in many ways.

Carmine had opened my eyes to a world of possibilities, and I was ready to seize them with both hands. Our mentorship hadn't ended with his revelation; it had evolved into something deeper, something more profound. It was a journey of self-discovery, of growth, and of becoming the best version of myself.

As I left Carmine's office that day, I felt a renewed sense of purpose, a burning desire to make a difference in the world. The world of finance was still a cutthroat arena, but I was armed not just with knowledge but with the wisdom to use it wisely.

The path ahead would be challenging, and the obstacles would be many. But I was no longer defined by my past mistakes; I was defined by my determination to overcome them. Carmine had shown me that life was a series of peaks and valleys, and it was up to me to climb those peaks and rise above those valleys.

And so, with Carmine's wisdom as my guide and my community as my inspiration, I embarked on a new journey—a journey to redefine success, to shatter the barriers that had held me back, and to create a legacy that went beyond wealth and power.

The adventure was far from over; in fact, it was just beginning. But I was ready, armed with the lessons and insights that Carmine had bestowed upon me. The future was uncertain, but one thing was clear—I was determined to make it an adventure worth living.

CHAPTER 18

THE RESILIENCE OF A DREAMER

As I stood at the crossroads of my life, I couldn't help but reflect on the tumultuous journey that had brought me to this moment. It had been a journey marked by trials and tribulations, by unexpected detours and painful setbacks. But above all, it had been a journey defined by one thing—resilience.

The audacious dream of becoming a stockbroker on Wall Street had ignited a fire within me, a fire that refused to be extinguished by the shadows of my past. I had faced countless obstacles, from the stain of a felony conviction to the challenges of intern life with a meager paycheck. But every hurdle had only fueled my determination to succeed.

My time on Wall Street had been a whirlwind of experiences, a rollercoaster ride through the highs and lows of the financial world. I had learned from the best, from the likes of Carmine, a mentor whose ruthless pursuit of excellence had left an indelible mark on me. In the face of adversity, I had not only survived but thrived, a testament to my unwavering spirit.

Carmine had delivered the crushing news that I could not become a stockbroker due to my felony. It had been a devastating blow, a dream slipping through my grasp. Yet, in that moment of despair, I had discovered a wealth far greater than any material riches—wisdom. It was a treasure I carried with me, a beacon of light in the darkest of times.

The corporate culture of Wall Street had been ruthless, driven by the mantra of "What would Carmine do?" But I had seen through the façade of materialism and greed. I had witnessed the transformation of Peanut and Billy, high school dropouts with no future, into success stories of their own making. It was a testament to the power of mentorship, of someone believing in your potential when you couldn't see it yourself.

My journey had taken me from the depths of despair to the

pinnacle of hope. I had faced racial profiling, injustice, and incarceration, but I had emerged stronger and more determined than ever. The resilience of a dreamer was a force to be reckoned with, a spirit that refused to be broken.

CHAPTER 19

ALWAYS BE CLOSING

As I closed the chapter on this part of my life, I couldn't help but look ahead with anticipation. The challenges and victories that lay on the horizon were unknown, but I welcomed them with open arms. My mission was clear—to rewrite the rules of wealth creation, to uplift my community, and to effect positive change in an industry that often lacked ethics and morality.

In the darkness of the night, as the city lights flickered, I knew that my journey was far from over. The world was a vast canvas, waiting for me to paint my story upon it. I had learned that wealth was not merely measured in dollars and cents, but in the lives we touched and the impact we made.

I had been a dreamer, and I would continue to be one—a dreamer with the audacity to chase dreams that seemed impossible, a dreamer with the resilience to overcome any obstacle, and a dreamer with the determination to rewrite the rules and inspire others to do the same.

And so, as I walked away from Wall Street, I left behind the trappings of materialism and embraced a new path—one that led to financial freedom not just for myself but for my people. It was a path illuminated by the light of wisdom, a path where ethics and integrity guided every step.

In the end, my story was not just my own—it was a testament to the power of resilience, determination, and the unwavering belief that audacious dreams could become reality. It was my hope that someone, somewhere, would be inspired by my journey, that they too would dare to dream, and in doing so, they would discover the incredible resilience of a dreamer.

As I walked into the night, the city's heartbeat pulsating around me, I knew that the adventure continued. The challenges and victories awaited, and I was ready to face them head-on. For I was Ernie G, the dreamer, the resilient, and the unwavering believer in the limitless possibilities that life had to offer.

PART 3

MOVIN' ON UP!

CHAPTER 20

THE AWAKENING

Vacation—the very word conjured images of sandy beaches, crystal-clear waters, and leisurely days spent without a care in the world. It was a luxury I had come to appreciate, not just for the relaxation it offered but for the freedom it represented.

I reclined in a plush beach chair, my toes buried in the warm sand, and my sunglasses perched on the bridge of my nose. The sun kissed my skin, and a gentle breeze rustled the pages of the novel in my hand. This was the life, a life I had worked tirelessly to achieve.

You see, I had unlocked a secret, a power that allowed me to make money whenever I wanted, as much as I wanted. I wasn't just a businessman; I was the businessman. I had the ability to create markets at will, to manipulate them like a master puppeteer. Wall Street had been my training ground, and now, I was the puppeteer, pulling the strings of wealth and power.

But even as I basked in the glorious fruits of my labor, the news I received was like a dark cloud looming over my paradise. Carmine, my mentor and the man who had been my guiding light on Wall Street, had passed away.

Carmine had been an enigmatic figure, a force of nature in a world where power and wealth were the ultimate currency. At the age of 40, he had it all—a thriving career, a loving family, a successful team of brokers, and wealth beyond imagination. He was the epitome of success, a symbol of prosperity. Yet, he had met his end, leaving behind a legacy that seemed too incredible to be real.
I stared out at the endless expanse of the ocean, the waves crashing against the shore in a never-ending cycle. I couldn't help but reflect on my own journey, the dreams and aspirations that had driven me to this point. Carmine's death served as a stark reminder that life was fragile, that even the mightiest could fall.
As I lay on the beach, the sand between my fingers, I couldn't help but think of the twists and turns that had brought me to

this moment. I had faced adversity head-on, and it had shaped me into the person I had become. The path to my dreams had taken unexpected detours, but I had emerged stronger and more resilient.

Carmine's death had served as a catalyst, a wake-up call. It was a reminder that life was too short to be wasted on the pursuit of wealth and power alone.

With a renewed sense of purpose, I made a decision. I would use all the skills and wealth principles I had learned on Wall Street to not just survive but to thrive in a new venture. It was time to chart a different course, to become the most powerful financier my city had ever seen.
The birth of an idea was the first step in this new journey. I conceived the notion of a marketing agency, one that specialized in financial education. It wasn't just about making money; it was about empowering others with the knowledge and tools to shape their financial destinies. I saw the potential for transformation, not just in my own life, but in the lives of countless others.
Of course, the path to this new vision was fraught with challenges. Starting a business from scratch was no easy feat. I faced financial constraints, the daunting task of finding clients, and the intricate process of setting up the agency. It was a whirlwind of paperwork, late nights, and countless cups of coffee. But amid the chaos and uncertainty, I secured my first client—a young couple seeking financial guidance. Their trust in me marked a significant milestone, a validation of my vision. It was a small step, but it was the beginning of something much larger.

As I gazed out at the endless horizon, I couldn't help but smile. My journey was just beginning, and I was filled with a sense of purpose and determination. I was ready to face the challenges that lay ahead, to use my knowledge and wealth to uplift my community and effect positive change in the finance industry.

With the sun setting on the horizon, I knew that the darkness of the night would give way to a new day, a day filled with possibilities and opportunities. I was ready to seize them all, to rewrite the rules of wealth creation, and to become the financial conqueror I was destined to be.

CHAPTER 21

THE RISE OF A LEADER

As the morning sun painted the sky with shades of gold and amber, I stood on the balcony of my sprawling estate, taking in the picturesque view that had become a symbol of my success. It was a view that had come to represent more than just a beautiful panorama—it symbolized the culmination of years of hard work, relentless determination, and a hunger for excellence.

My success was undeniable, and it manifested in the Rolls-Royce Phantom that graced my driveway, the sleek Tesla Model X that my wife, Yelissa, drove, and the grandeur of our spacious home that boasted a view of the city skyline. But my achievements were not limited to material possessions; they extended to the reputation I had earned as a leader and mentor.

You see, I had a knack for creating leaders, a talent that had earned me a formidable reputation in my community. It was a reputation that I had cultivated through years of experience, first in the military and then on Wall Street, where I had honed my leadership skills to perfection.

In the Navy, I had learned the value of discipline, determination, and unwavering commitment. These traits had propelled me through the ranks at an astonishing pace, and I had emerged as a leader among my peers. The military had provided me with the structure and training needed to excel, and I had thrived in that environment.

My time on Wall Street had been equally transformative. It was a world of high-stakes finance, a place where fortunes were made and lost in the blink of an eye. But I had thrived in that chaotic arena, using my military-honed discipline to navigate the treacherous waters of the financial industry. The blend of military precision and Wall Street acumen had transformed me into an elite financier, a master of wealth creation, and a mentor to those who sought my guidance. I was living proof that success could be achieved through hard work, dedication, and a commitment to personal growth.

My marketing agency, specializing in financial education, had flourished beyond my wildest dreams. Clients from diverse backgrounds sought our services, driven by a thirst for knowledge and a desire to take control of their financial futures. It was a testament to the power of education and empowerment. But behind every successful man stands a woman of equal strength and grace. Yelissa, my loving wife, was the pillar of support that had enabled my achievements. Her unwavering belief in my vision, her dedication to our family, and her grace under pressure had been instrumental in our journey to success.

Yelissa was not just the woman I loved; she was my partner in every sense of the word. Her intelligence and financial acumen complemented my own, making us a formidable team. It was her Tesla Model X that greeted me each day as a symbol of our shared success.

Our family life was a testament to the balance we had achieved. I had initiated free financial education workshops and mentorship programs for our neighbors, recognizing that our success had the potential to uplift an entire community. It was a way to bridge the gap between generations of poverty and a brighter future, one defined by financial literacy and empowerment.

As the founder of my marketing agency and the driving force behind these community initiatives, I had undergone a transformation. My vision had evolved beyond individual success. I saw the potential to create a community of financially savvy individuals, individuals who could break free from the cycle of poverty and build a legacy of their own.

I had become a beacon of hope, a source of inspiration, and a solution to the challenges that had plagued my community for generations. The skills and knowledge I had acquired in the military and on Wall Street were now tools I used to empower others. I reveled in the role of mentorship, guiding individuals on their own journeys to financial success. I saw potential in each person I encountered, and I was determined to help them unlock it. My reputation as a financial mentor and leader in the community continued to grow, cementing my position as a force for positive change. But my journey was far from over. The challenges that lay ahead were as formidable as those I had already conquered, but I was prepared to face them head-on. My vision extended beyond the confines of our community; it encompassed a world where financial literacy was not a privilege but a right.

With each sunrise, I was reminded that there was much work to be done. I had become a leader, not just of individuals, but of a movement—a movement that aimed to rewrite the rules of wealth creation, to redefine success, and to empower those who had been marginalized for far too long.

As I looked out over the city, I couldn't help but smile. My journey had brought me to this point, and there was no turning back. The road ahead was illuminated by the possibilities of transformation, and I was ready to lead the way.

CHAPTER 22

WEALTH PRINCIPLES

In the world of Wall Street, where fortunes are made and lost in the blink of an eye, I learned invaluable wealth principles that would later become the cornerstone of my financial success. These principles aren't just about making money; they're about understanding the profound impact that money can have on our lives and the lives of those around us. So, let me share with you five key wealth principles that have guided me on my journey.

Principle 1: Only Spend Money on Things That Increase, Not Decrease in Value

Imagine you're walking through a mall, and you come across a shiny new sports car. It's tempting, isn't it? But here's the first wealth principle: only spend money on things that increase, not decrease in value. That sports car might make you feel good temporarily, but it's not an investment; it's an expense.

In my Wall Street days, I saw people make this mistake all the time. They spent their hard-earned money on flashy items that had no lasting value. Instead, I learned to invest in assets that appreciate over time. Stocks, real estate, businesses—these are the things that can grow your wealth. So, before you make a purchase, ask yourself if it will increase in value or if it's just a temporary thrill.

Principle 2: Money Is a Means, Not a Goal

Money is a tool, not the ultimate goal. It's a means to an end, a way to achieve your dreams and provide security for your family. Too often, people get caught up in the pursuit of wealth for its own sake. They make money their primary goal, and in doing so, they lose sight of what truly matters.

In my journey, I learned that money should serve your goals and aspirations, not the other way around. It's a tool that can help you live the life you want, support causes you believe in, and create a better future for yourself and your loved ones. So, always remember that money is a means to an end, not the end itself.

Principle 3: Money Is Not Evil or Good Unless You Make It So

Money is often given a bad reputation, as if it's inherently evil. But here's the truth: money is neither good nor evil. It's simply a reflection of the choices we make with it. Some people use money to do terrible things, while others use it to make the world a better place.

I learned this principle from the diverse group of people I encountered on Wall Street. Money can magnify your character, so it's essential to use it responsibly and ethically. You can choose to make a positive impact with your wealth, whether it's through philanthropy, supporting causes you believe in, or simply being generous to those in need. So, remember that money is a neutral force; it's your actions that determine its moral value.

Principle 4: Money Is a Tool

Money is a tool—a powerful one at that. It can help you achieve your goals, whether they're financial, personal, or philanthropic. But like any tool, it requires skill and knowledge to use effectively.

Think of it this way: if you had a toolbox full of advanced tools, you wouldn't use them without understanding how they work, right? The same goes for money. It's essential to educate yourself about financial principles, investing strategies, and wealth management. Take the time to learn how to make your money work for you.

Principle 5: The Art of Rebuilding

Life is full of unexpected twists and turns. Sometimes, despite all your efforts, you can lose everything. It happened to me, and it's a lesson I carry with me every day. But here's the thing about successful hustlers: they can lose it all and get it right back.

When you hit rock bottom and rebuild from scratch, you gain a wisdom that no amount of success can teach. It's about resilience, adaptability, and the ability to rise from the ashes with newfound strength.

So, remember that it's not about how many times life knocks you down; it's about how many times you get back up. Embrace the art of rebuilding, armed with the wisdom you've gained along the way.

These wealth principles aren't just about making money; they're about creating a future that's not only financially secure but also fulfilling and meaningful. Use them as your guide on your journey to financial success and personal growth.

CHAPTER 23

THE FINANCIAL METROPOLIS

I stood at the heart of a bustling metropolis, one that had undergone a profound transformation. It wasn't just about the towering skyscrapers or the glittering lights that illuminated the night sky. The real transformation was in the people, the community that had once been plagued by poverty, crime, and despair. As I gazed out at the thriving neighborhood that had emerged from the ashes, I couldn't help but feel a sense of pride and accomplishment. This was the result of years of hard work, dedication, and a belief in the power of financial education.

The changes had been dramatic. Crime rates had plummeted, giving residents a newfound sense of safety. Educational opportunities had expanded, with scholarships and mentorship programs providing young minds with the tools they needed to succeed. Job opportunities were on the rise, and the local economy was flourishing. But this transformation wasn't just about economics and statistics. It was about hope, resilience, and the belief that a brighter future was possible for everyone in the community. Yet, as with any great story, there was one final challenge, a formidable obstacle that threatened to undo all the progress we had made. A powerful conglomerate had set its sights on our neighborhood, seeking to exploit our newfound prosperity for its gain.

Their plans were ruthless. They aimed to push out long-time residents and strip away the very essence of our community. It was a battle between corporate greed and the resilience of the people. The showdown was inevitable. I knew that if we didn't stand up to this conglomerate, all our hard work would be in vain. It was time to put my financial expertise to the test, to use everything I had learned on Wall Street to protect the community's newfound wealth.

I called upon a team of experts, each with their own unique skills, to help me uncover the conglomerate's unethical practices. We delved into their financial records, exposed their shady dealings, and laid bare their intentions to the public. What we uncovered was a web of deceit and exploitation. SterlingCorp had been using legal loopholes to squeeze every penny out of our community. It was corporate greed at its worst.

Our next move was crucial. Armed with irrefutable evidence of SterlingCorp's unethical practices, Ernie orchestrated a public meeting in our neighborhood park. The media was invited to ensure our message reached every corner of the city.

Ernie stood on a makeshift stage, the crowd's collective anger palpable. In his hands, he held the evidence that would expose SterlingCorp's dirty secrets. With eloquence and precision, he presented our findings, detailing the conglomerate's exploitative schemes. The crowd listened intently, anger simmering in their eyes.

The confrontation was high-stakes, a battle not just for financial prosperity but for the soul of our community. The conglomerate's leaders were formidable opponents, but I was armed with knowledge, and knowledge is a powerful weapon. In a tense meeting, I confronted the conglomerate's leaders, laying out the evidence of their wrongdoing for all to see. They squirmed in their seats, but I didn't back down. I knew that the principles we stood for were far more significant than their lust for profit. The community rallied behind me , united by a common purpose—to protect the future we had worked so hard to build.

In the end, we emerged victorious. The conglomerate was exposed, and justice was served. Our community remained intact, stronger than ever, a testament to the power of unity and the unwavering belief that prosperity should benefit all, not just a privileged few.

As I stood there, looking out at the city I had helped transform, I knew that our journey was far from over. There would always be challenges to face and obstacles to overcome. But armed with the wisdom we had gained and the resilience of our community, I was confident that we could face whatever lay ahead.

Our financial metropolis was a symbol of what was possible when people came together, armed with knowledge and a shared vision of a better future. And as we moved forward, I couldn't help but feel a sense of hope and optimism for the days to come.

The Financial Conqueror, as they called me, had become more than just a name. It was a symbol of what one person, armed with the right principles and a community of supporters, could achieve. And our story was far from over—it was just the beginning of a new chapter in our journey towards prosperity, justice, and a brighter future for all.

CHAPTER 24

THE UNFINISHED SYMPHONY

The battle was over. The dust had settled, and victory stood firmly on our side. SterlingCorp, the formidable conglomerate that had threatened to devour our neighborhood, lay defeated. It had been a long and arduous journey, but it was a journey that had solidified my legacy as the greatest financier the world had ever known.

As I stood amidst the cheers and applause of my neighbors, I couldn't help but feel a sense of profound accomplishment. The conglomerate had underestimated our determination, our unity, and our unwavering spirit. In a showdown of principles, we had emerged victorious. The media coverage of SterlingCorp's unethical practices had tarnished their reputation beyond repair, and their financial losses were insurmountable.

I had used every skill and wealth principle I had learned on Wall Street to defeat this formidable adversary. The knowledge that money was a tool, not a goal, had guided our strategy. We had hit SterlingCorp where it hurt the most—their profits. Boycotting businesses with ties to the conglomerate had weakened their grip on our community while strengthening our own economy. The battle had been as much about strategy as it was about determination, and we had executed both flawlessly. Our neighborhood had been transformed into a symbol of resilience and financial empowerment. Crime rates had plummeted, educational opportunities had risen, and our streets bustled with thriving businesses. The once-struggling community was now a testament to our dedication.

I had seen my neighbors' lives change before my eyes. Families that had once lived paycheck to paycheck were now investing in their futures. Young entrepreneurs had sprung up, fueled by their newfound financial knowledge. Our community had become a beacon of hope, a place where dreams were not just realized but exceeded. One of the greatest joys of victory was watching the next generation thrive. As a mentor, I had instilled in them the importance of financial knowledge and discipline. They had embraced these lessons with open arms, and it was evident in their success. The idea of generational wealth, once a distant dream, was now a reality for many families in our neighborhood.

It was a powerful feeling to witness parents passing down financial wisdom to their children. The cycle of poverty had been broken, replaced by a cycle of prosperity. Our community was no longer just surviving; it was thriving, and it was doing so because we had all stood together.

As I sat in my office, surrounded by the trappings of success—a desk overlooking the bustling streets of our neighborhood, a view of the thriving businesses, and the sounds of children playing in the park—I couldn't help but reflect on the incredible journey that had brought me here.

My path had taken me from the disciplined world of the Navy to the cutthroat environment of Wall Street. I had faced rejection and disappointment, but I had also experienced the thrill of success. I had climbed the ranks, not just as a financier but as a leader. My reputation for creating leaders was well-earned, and I was proud to see so many of my mentees flourishing.

I had learned the wealth principles that had guided me throughout my journey. Money was a tool, not a goal. It could be used for both good and ill, and it was up to us to determine its purpose. Money was neither evil nor good; it was our choices that defined its morality. I had understood that only by spending money on things that increased in value could we truly accumulate wealth. And I had lived by the principle that life was filled with peaks and valleys, understanding that every setback was an opportunity for growth.

My story, a rollercoaster of determination, community, and financial wisdom, served as an inspiration for others. I had rewritten my destiny, transformed a struggling neighborhood into a financial metropolis, and left a legacy of prosperity. It was a testament to the power of chasing one's dreams and embracing financial literacy. I had started this journey with a burning desire to create generational wealth, not just for myself but for my community. I had learned that wealth was not just about money;

it was about knowledge, resilience, and unity. It was about using our resources to uplift others and build a brighter future.

My community had become a shining example of what could be achieved when people came together with a common purpose. I looked out over the thriving financial metropolis we had created, I knew that our journey was only just beginning. There were more challenges to face, more lives to transform, and more dreams to be realized. But with determination, unity, and the wisdom of financial literacy, there was no obstacle too great, no mountain too high.
The legacy of prosperity would continue, one community, one family, one dream at a time.

CHAPTER 25

THE LEGACY CONTINUES

I found myself at the head of a massive boardroom table, surrounded by the most influential figures in the financial industry. Their eyes were fixed on me, hanging on to every word that escaped my lips. It was a scene I could have never imagined during my early days in the Navy, and it was a testament to the incredible journey I had undertaken.

As I looked around the room, I couldn't help but feel a profound sense of gratitude for the path that had led me here. The lessons I had learned, the community I had built, and the determination that had driven me forward—all of it had culminated in this very moment.

My speech echoed with the wisdom of a man who had not just achieved financial success but had also empowered countless others to do the same. I spoke of the wealth principles that had guided me throughout my life and how they had transformed not only my destiny but the destiny of an entire community.

I told them of my days in the Navy, where I had learned the virtues of discipline, honor, and commitment—virtues that had laid the foundation for my success. My time on Wall Street had honed my financial acumen, teaching me that money was a tool, not a goal. I had shared stories of the struggles I faced, the rejection that had fueled my determination, and the moments of triumph that had made it all worthwhile.

As I spoke, I could see the faces of those in the audience, individuals who had overcome their own challenges, entrepreneurs who had embraced financial literacy, and leaders who had taken their communities to new heights. They were living proof of the transformative power of determination and unity.

My story was not just about me; it was about the countless lives I had touched, the families I had helped secure generational wealth, and the community that had risen from the ashes of poverty to become a financial metropolis. It was a story of rewriting destinies, transforming lives, and leaving a legacy of prosperity. And as I concluded my speech, the room erupted into applause. The message had resonated with everyone present, a reminder that anyone, regardless of their background or circumstances, could be anything they wanted to be. If I could do it, anyone could.

Now, you might be wondering where I find myself today. I stand before you as a man who has achieved more than he ever dreamed possible. I'm not just a financier; I'm a leader, a mentor, and a symbol of what can be achieved when we come together with a common purpose.

I continue to lead my marketing agency specializing in financial education, but it's more than just a business; it's a movement. We've expanded our reach far beyond our neighborhood, impacting communities across the country. Financial literacy has become a fundamental part of our educational system, ensuring that every child has the tools they need to secure their financial future. I've also become an advocate for financial reform, pushing for regulations that protect the vulnerable from the predatory practices of corporate giants. It's a battle I've fought with the same determination that guided me through the darkest days of my life. But my greatest joy comes from watching the next generation thrive. I see young entrepreneurs, armed with financial knowledge and determination, rising to new heights. Families are passing down the wisdom of financial literacy, ensuring that generational wealth is not just a dream but a reality.

CONCLUSION

So, where can you find me now?

You can find me in boardrooms like this one, sharing my story, my wisdom, and my passion for financial empowerment. You can find me in communities across the nation, working tirelessly to rewrite destinies and transform lives. And you can find me in the hearts and minds of those who refuse to accept the limitations society places upon them.

My journey is far from over, and the legacy of prosperity continues. I am living proof that with determination, unity, and the wisdom of financial literacy, there is no obstacle too great, no mountain too high. And I stand before you as a reminder that you can be anything you want to be.

If I could do it, anyone can.

ABOUT THE AUTHOR

Ernest E Goethe

The author, hailing from the vibrant city of Newark, New Jersey, brings a rich tapestry of experiences to "Ernie G's Dream: The Hidden Truth of Wall Street." As an honorably discharged veteran, he has not only served his country with distinction but also carried those values of discipline and integrity into the world of business. Currently, he stands at the helm of his own successful enterprise, embodying the very principles of entrepreneurship and perseverance that this book explores. Beyond his achievements in the business world, he is a passionate advocate for the economic empowerment and revitalization of his community, a mission that resonates deeply throughout the pages of his work. His unique blend of personal experience, financial expertise, and a commitment to uplifting his community shines through in this captivating narrative, making "Ernie G's Dream" not only an insightful exploration of Wall Street but also a testament to his dedication to improving the lives of those around him.

Made in the USA
Middletown, DE
03 November 2023